The Starlight Sleigh

The Starlight Sleigh

Matthew Petchinsky

The Starlight Sleigh: A Holiday Journey
By: Matthew Petchinsky

Introduction: The Legend of the Starlight Sleigh

In the vast expanse of the cosmos, where galaxies dance in the endless dark, there exists a tale whispered across the stars—a tale of hope, joy, and the unyielding magic of the Starlight Sleigh. Far beyond the bounds of Earth, this extraordinary sleigh does not merely deliver gifts to children tucked into their beds on Christmas Eve. No, its mission is far greater, far more wondrous. The Starlight Sleigh brings light to the darkest corners of the universe, weaving threads of joy, hope, and love into the very fabric of existence.

Legends speak of its creation, a gift from the celestial beings themselves, forged in the fires of a dying star. The sleigh shimmered like liquid silver, with intricate carvings of constellations glowing faintly upon its surface, each representing a promise of kindness. Powered by the essence of starlight, it glided effortlessly across the cosmos, traversing not only physical realms but the intangible landscapes of dreams and hearts. It was a beacon of unity, a testament to the interconnectedness of all life, wherever it may flourish.

Guided by the brightest star in the heavens—aptly named Lumina Solis—the Starlight Sleigh drew its power from the star's eternal brilliance. The bond between the sleigh and its guiding light was unbreakable, a sacred connection that symbolized the endless cycle of giving and renewal. For centuries, it carried out its cosmic mission, overseen by a timeless caretaker who became the universe's herald of joy: the Astral Claus.

But as with all legends, this one bore its share of darkness. One fateful Christmas Eve, as the Starlight Sleigh soared through the galactic expanse, Lumina Solis faltered. Without warning or reason, the brightest star dimmed, its light extinguished as though consumed by an unseen force. The Starlight Sleigh came to an abrupt halt, its magic dissipating like mist in the morning sun. The universe seemed to hold its breath, mourning the loss of its celestial guardian.

For years, the sleigh remained dormant, an empty vessel of untapped potential. Across planets, whispers spread of its fall. Some said it was a punishment for taking its power for granted. Others believed it was a test, a challenge to prove that the spirit of giving and hope could endure even without divine guidance. Whatever the cause, the cosmos felt the void left by the Starlight Sleigh. Wars erupted in places once harmonious, stars faded prematurely, and despair seeped into corners where it had never before dwelled.

Yet even in the depths of loss, there were those who believed. These dreamers refused to let the light of Lumina Solis fade completely from memory. They carried its legend in their hearts, telling the tale to their children, passing it down through generations, and keeping alive the hope that one day the sleigh would rise again.

This story begins in such a time, when the legend of the Starlight Sleigh is little more than a myth to most. The Astral Claus, now old and weary, clings to his last spark of belief. He knows that the Starlight Sleigh's magic cannot be reignited without a new source of light, a star born not of the cosmos, but of the hearts of those who still believe in the power of hope, love, and selfless giving.

As the universe teeters on the edge of darkness, an extraordinary journey unfolds—a quest to find the new guiding star that will restore the sleigh's brilliance and, with it, the joy and unity of the cosmos. This is not merely a tale of Christmas; it is a tale of resilience, of how the smallest acts of kindness can light the way through the deepest shadows.

The Starlight Sleigh awaits. Its journey is far from over, and its story is about to begin anew. Will you join the quest to restore its light? Will you become the spark that reignites the brightest star? The cosmos is watching, waiting, and hoping. Let the legend of the Starlight Sleigh inspire you to believe in the magic of giving once more.

Chapter 1: The Broken Sleigh

In the quiet, snow-draped town of Evergreen Hollow, life moved at a pace as unhurried as the snowfall on Christmas Eve. Tucked into the hills and surrounded by an ancient forest, the town seemed forgotten by time, its streets lined with gas lamps and charming brick facades. At the edge of town stood a rambling old farm, long abandoned and whispered to be haunted by children with more imagination than sense. It was here, on an unremarkable winter morning, that the ordinary lives of Max and Clara Wilkes began to intertwine with a story that would reshape the cosmos.

Max, a young inventor with a mind constantly buzzing with ideas, was well-known for tinkering with machines that no one else could fix—or so much as understand. His small workshop was cluttered with half-built gadgets, gears, and blueprints, all of which seemed to overflow into the modest home he shared with his sister Clara. Clara, younger by two years, was the practical one, her imagination rivaling Max's but tempered by a deep sense of responsibility. If Max dreamed up fantastical contraptions, Clara made sure they didn't explode.

That morning, Max had been drawn to the old farm by rumors of an "unbreakable lock" securing the barn doors, a challenge that set his curiosity ablaze. Clara tagged along reluctantly, bundled in her thick coat and scarf, muttering about how they should be helping decorate for the town's Christmas festival instead. Max, however, was undeterred.

The barn loomed before them, its weathered timbers darkened by decades of storms. Snow clung to its slanted roof, and icicles hung like crystal teeth from its eaves. Max worked on the lock with a pick he'd made himself, a device of springs and levers that he called his "key-ina-tor." With a satisfying click, the rusted padlock fell away, and the massive doors creaked open, revealing shadows and silence.

Inside, dust motes swirled in the beams of pale light that filtered through cracks in the walls. At first, there was nothing remarkable about the barn. Its interior was filled with the usual detritus of farm life: broken tools, rotted barrels, and heaps of straw. But then Max's gaze landed on something extraordinary at the far end of the barn.

Covered in a heavy tarp, the object exuded an unexplainable aura, as though the air around it shimmered with faint traces of warmth and light. Max approached, heart pounding, and with Clara's hesitant help, he pulled back the tarp.

What lay beneath was unlike anything they'd ever seen. The sleigh was sleek and magnificent, though tarnished with age and neglect. Its metal surface was etched with delicate constellations that seemed to glimmer faintly, even in the dim light. It was enormous, far larger than any sleigh meant for earthly roads, and its runners curved gracefully as if designed to glide through both snow and stars.

"This... this is no ordinary sleigh," Clara whispered, her breath visible in the frigid air.

Max was already examining the intricate carvings and mechanisms, his fingers tracing the symbols as though they spoke to him. But before he could respond, a deep, resonant voice echoed from the shadows behind them.

"You're right, Clara. It isn't."

The siblings whirled around to see a figure step into the light. He was impossibly tall, his presence commanding yet kind. His white beard flowed like fresh-fallen snow, and his crimson coat was lined with starlight that seemed to flicker as he moved. Though older and wearier than any portrayal they'd ever seen, there was no mistaking who stood before them.

"Santa?" Clara stammered, her voice barely audible.

He nodded solemnly, his eyes filled with a profound sadness. "You've found the Starlight Sleigh, the greatest treasure of the cosmos... and my greatest failure."

Santa explained that the sleigh had been dormant for decades, ever since the Star of Unity—the celestial gem that powered it—had vanished. The Star of Unity was no ordinary jewel; it was a fragment of creation itself, imbued with the combined hope and joy of every heart across the universe. Without it, the sleigh's magic had faded, and Santa had been grounded, confined to earthly means of delivering Christmas cheer.

"Without the sleigh, I can't reach the farthest corners of the universe. I can't bring hope to the places that need it most," Santa confessed, his voice heavy with the weight of years.

Max's mind raced with possibilities. "But if we find the Star of Unity, we can restore the sleigh, right?"

Santa smiled faintly, the first glimmer of hope breaking through his weariness. "Yes, but it won't be easy. The Star of Unity isn't just lost—it's hidden. Its light can only be rekindled by those who truly believe in the power of hope and giving. The journey to find it will test your courage, your ingenuity, and your hearts."

Clara hesitated, glancing at her brother. "Why us? We're just... normal kids."

"You're far from ordinary," Santa said, his gaze warm and knowing. "Max, your inventions come from a place of boundless imagination, and Clara, your heart is a beacon of compassion. Together, you embody the qualities needed to restore the Star's light. I've been waiting for you two."

The enormity of the task settled over them like freshly fallen snow, both exhilarating and daunting. Max looked back at the sleigh, its tarnished surface seeming to shimmer faintly as if responding to Santa's words.

"What do we do first?" Max asked, his voice steady with determination.

Santa's eyes twinkled with the faintest spark of his old magic. "First, we repair the sleigh. Its mechanisms are complex, but with your ingenuity, I believe it can fly again. After that, we'll need to follow the trail of the Star's light. It's faint, but it's out there, waiting to be found."

As Santa outlined the first steps of their journey, the barn seemed to come alive, the faint glow of the sleigh casting long shadows that danced like living starlight. Max and Clara exchanged a glance, their usual sibling banter replaced by a shared understanding: their lives would never be the same.

The legend of the Starlight Sleigh was no longer just a story—it was their story. And the universe was counting on them to bring its magic back.

Chapter 2: The Cosmic Call to Adventure

The night after discovering the Starlight Sleigh, Max and Clara lay restless in their beds, their minds racing with thoughts of the impossible. How could two small-town siblings be chosen for such an immense responsibility? Yet, the warmth in Santa's eyes and the gentle conviction in his voice made them believe, even if just a little, that they were meant for something greater. The next morning, before the sun rose, they found themselves back in the barn, their breath fogging in the frosty air as Santa stood beside the sleigh.

"We begin now," Santa declared, his voice steady and resolute. He ran a gloved hand over the tarnished metal of the sleigh, and for a brief moment, the constellations etched into its surface pulsed faintly with light. "The journey will take us beyond Earth, far into realms of magic and mystery. To restore the Star of Unity, we must retrieve its fragments, each imbued with an essential aspect of the Christmas spirit: giving, gratitude, love, and belief. Only when they are reunited will the Star shine again."

Max adjusted his scarf, trying to mask the nervous energy that churned in his chest. Clara stood close by, her brow furrowed with determination. "Where do we start?" she asked, her voice unwavering despite the uncertainty.

Santa stepped into the sleigh, motioning for them to follow. As they climbed aboard, the sleigh's interior shimmered with an otherworldly glow. A control panel with crystalline levers and a glowing compass sat at the front, humming softly with latent magic. Santa pulled a lever, and the sleigh shuddered to life, rising gently off the ground.

With a whoosh, the barn doors opened, and the sleigh shot into the sky, leaving behind the snowy fields of Evergreen Hollow. As they ascended, the world below faded, replaced by the infinite expanse of the cosmos. Stars blazed brighter than Max and Clara had ever imagined, their light weaving a tapestry of wonder across the void.

Their first destination appeared on the horizon: a swirling nebula of gold and crimson that pulsed like a living heart. Santa explained that this was the Realm of Giving, where the first fragment of the Star of Unity was hidden. The sleigh descended gently, landing on a shimmering platform of crystalline ice that sparkled with an inner light. As they stepped out, the air buzzed with energy, and a figure emerged from the swirling mist.

The figure was tall and radiant, cloaked in robes of shifting colors that seemed to reflect the hopes and dreams of every being in the universe. "Welcome, travelers," the celestial being said, their voice resonating like a symphony. "I am Aurelia, Keeper of Giving. To claim the fragment, you must prove your understanding of selfless generosity."

Aurelia raised a hand, and the mist around them solidified into a scene: a small village bathed in starlight, where families huddled together in modest homes. The villagers looked tired, their faces etched with worry, but their eyes held a flicker of hope. "These people need help," Aurelia said. "You must give, but only what is truly needed. Too much or too little, and their light will fade."

Max and Clara exchanged a glance. The task seemed simple, but as they moved through the village, they realized the complexity of true giving. One family needed food, but only enough to last until their crops could grow. Another needed tools, but only ones they could use with their limited knowledge. The siblings worked tirelessly, listening to the villagers' stories and understanding their needs.

When their work was done, Aurelia reappeared, a smile gracing her luminous face. "You have shown wisdom and compassion," she said, extending a glowing shard of light. "Take this fragment. It holds the essence of giving, the first step to restoring the Star of Unity."

With the fragment in hand, they returned to the sleigh, its interior glowing a little brighter as the shard was placed into a crystalline slot on the control panel. Santa nodded approvingly. "One down, three to go."

Their next destination was the Realm of Gratitude, a vast, glittering plane of golden sands that sparkled under a sky of ever-shifting auroras. The Keeper of Gratitude, a serene figure named Solara, greeted them with a challenge: to navigate a maze of mirrors, each reflecting their fears and doubts. Only by expressing genuine gratitude for their strengths and acknowledging their weaknesses could they find the exit.

The maze tested them in unexpected ways. Max faced his fear of failure, seeing countless reflections of himself struggling with unfinished inventions. Clara confronted her fear of being overshadowed, the mirrors showing her countless scenarios where her efforts went unnoticed. With Santa's guidance and their shared resolve, they found their way, learning to be grateful not only for their talents but for each other's unwavering support.

Emerging from the maze, Solara presented them with the second fragment, its golden light warm and steady. "Gratitude strengthens the spirit," she said. "Without it, the Star's light would falter."

Their journey continued to the Realm of Love, a vibrant, verdant world where every plant and creature radiated warmth and connection. Here, they met Lumis, a gentle Keeper who explained that the fragment could only be claimed by demonstrating love not just for others, but for themselves.

This challenge was the most difficult yet, requiring them to confront deeply buried insecurities. Max struggled to see his worth beyond his inventions, while Clara wrestled with her fear of being insignificant. Through heartfelt conversations and moments of vulnerability, they began to heal, their bond growing stronger with each revelation. Lumis, moved by their courage, gifted them the third fragment, its light pulsing like a heartbeat.

Finally, they reached the Realm of Belief, a stark, otherworldly landscape of shifting shadows and blinding light. Here, they met Astra, the Keeper of Belief, who challenged them to hold onto hope even as illusions tried to shatter their resolve. In a series of trials, they faced visions of failure, doubt, and despair, their belief in themselves and the mission tested to its limits.

When the trials ended, Astra revealed the final fragment, its light pure and unyielding. "Belief is the foundation of magic," Astra said. "Without it, the Star of Unity cannot shine."

As they returned to the sleigh, the four fragments merged into a single, radiant gem. The Star of Unity pulsed with life, filling the sleigh with a brilliant glow. Santa smiled, his eyes shimmering with tears of gratitude. "You've done it," he said, his voice thick with emotion. "The Star of Unity lives again."

Though their journey was far from over, Max and Clara felt a renewed sense of purpose. They had ventured beyond the bounds of Earth, faced unimaginable challenges, and emerged stronger together. With the Star of Unity restored, they were one step closer to reigniting the magic of the Starlight Sleigh—and bringing hope to the entire universe.

Chapter 3: The Frozen Nebula

The Starlight Sleigh soared deeper into the cosmos, leaving behind the glowing realms of giving, gratitude, love, and belief. Ahead lay the Frozen Nebula, a desolate expanse of ice and shadow where starlight struggled to penetrate. The nebula was infamous among celestial travelers, a place where even the bravest dared not linger. It was said to be a realm of unending frost, haunted by an ancient guardian whose icy heart knew neither warmth nor joy.

Max and Clara sat close together in the sleigh, their breaths misting in the frigid air. Santa guided the sleigh with quiet determination, but even he seemed subdued. The light of the Star of Unity, glowing faintly in its crystalline slot, seemed to dim as they neared their destination.

"Why is this place so cold?" Clara asked, her voice barely a whisper.

Santa glanced at her, his expression solemn. "The Frozen Nebula was not always like this. It was once a vibrant realm, filled with light and life. But centuries ago, its guardian, the Ice Warden, turned bitter and isolated. The nebula reflects the Warden's heart—cold, desolate, and unyielding."

"Why did the Warden become that way?" Max asked, leaning forward.

Santa sighed deeply. "Loneliness. Betrayal. Pain. The Warden once trusted deeply but was abandoned in their time of need. Instead of healing, they allowed their pain to consume them, freezing everything around them. The final fragment of the Star of Unity is hidden here, but the Warden guards it fiercely. To retrieve it, we must thaw their heart."

The sleigh began its descent, landing on a vast, frozen plain of cracked ice and jagged frost spires. The air was eerily still, save for the faint howling of a distant wind. Above them, the nebula's swirling colors were muted, like a once-vivid painting now faded and worn.

As they stepped out of the sleigh, the cold bit at their faces, sharper than any winter night they had ever known. Clara pulled her scarf tighter, and Max adjusted the straps on his pack, which contained tools he thought might be useful. Santa walked ahead, his crimson coat a stark contrast against the white and gray expanse.

Suddenly, the ground beneath them rumbled, and a massive figure emerged from the icy mist. The Ice Warden stood before them, towering and formidable, encased in armor of shimmering frost. Their eyes, pale and piercing, glowed with an otherworldly light. The Warden's voice was like the grinding of glaciers, deep and unyielding.

"Who dares trespass in my realm?" the Warden demanded, their words echoing across the frozen plain.

Santa stepped forward, his posture firm but respectful. "We come seeking the final fragment of the Star of Unity. The universe needs its light restored, and only you can help us retrieve it."

The Warden laughed, a sound as cold as the wind that whipped around them. "Help you? Why should I? The universe abandoned me long ago. Let it remain in darkness, as I have."

Max felt a pang of sympathy for the Warden, but Clara stepped forward, her voice steady. "We know what it's like to feel alone, to think no one understands or cares. But shutting everyone out doesn't make the pain go away. It only makes it worse."

The Warden's eyes narrowed, their icy gaze locking onto Clara. "You presume to know my pain, child? My trust was shattered, my heart betrayed. I was left to freeze while the rest of the cosmos thrived. Why should I forgive? Why should I let anyone in?"

Santa placed a hand on Clara's shoulder, signaling her to step back. "Because forgiveness is the first step toward healing," he said gently. "The universe has not forgotten you, Warden. Your pain matters, but so does your ability to rise above it. You were once a protector of light. That part of you is still there, waiting to be rekindled."

The Warden hesitated, their icy armor cracking faintly as if the weight of Santa's words struck something deep within. But the frost around them grew sharper, the air colder. "Prove your worth," the Warden said. "If you seek the fragment, then show me the strength of your belief in the warmth of community."

With a wave of their hand, the Warden conjured a massive ice labyrinth, its walls shimmering with frost and its passages twisting endlessly. "Within this maze lies the fragment. You must navigate it together. But beware—this labyrinth reflects your doubts, your fears, and your failures. Only by working as one will you find the way."

The labyrinth's entrance yawned before them, its icy threshold glowing faintly. Max, Clara, and Santa exchanged determined glances before stepping inside. The cold seemed to intensify with each step, and the walls pulsed faintly, as if alive.

Almost immediately, the labyrinth began to play tricks on their minds. Clara found herself separated from the others, wandering alone through passages that seemed to shift and close behind her. Visions of her greatest fears appeared in the ice: being forgotten, overshadowed, and left behind.

Max faced his own trial, the walls reflecting his insecurities as an inventor. He saw scenes of failure, of his creations breaking apart and people laughing at his ideas. The weight of self-doubt pressed heavily on him, threatening to freeze him in place.

Santa, too, faced his burden—the memories of those he could not reach, the faces of children who had lost hope during the years the sleigh was grounded. The guilt threatened to overwhelm him, the ice around him growing thicker.

But as they each struggled, they began to hear faint echoes of one another's voices. Clara's determination to find Max and Santa pushed her forward. Max's resolve to protect Clara ignited a spark of confidence. Santa's enduring faith in them both melted the edges of his guilt.

Finally, they reunited at the heart of the labyrinth, where a single shard of light glowed within a pedestal of ice. The Warden appeared, their icy form shimmering. "You have found the fragment," the Warden said, their voice softer now. "But tell me—why should I trust you with it?"

Max stepped forward, his breath visible in the cold air. "Because we didn't make it here alone. We made it because we believed in each other, even when things felt impossible. That's what you've been missing—community. Let us help you thaw the ice around your heart."

Clara added, "You don't have to be alone anymore. Let us show you the warmth you've been missing."

For a long moment, the Warden was silent. Then, cracks began to spread across their icy armor, light spilling through the fractures. With a final shudder, the armor shattered, revealing a figure of radiant starlight. The Warden's true form glowed with warmth and life, their eyes now soft and luminous.

"You have reminded me of who I once was," the Warden said, extending the fragment toward them. "Take this, and let its light guide you. Thank you for showing me the power of forgiveness and community."

As the fragment joined the others in the sleigh, the Frozen Nebula began to change. The frost melted, revealing vibrant, shimmering landscapes beneath. Stars shone brighter, and the air grew warmer. The Warden bowed in gratitude, their once-lonely heart now rekindled.

Max, Clara, and Santa returned to the sleigh, their spirits soaring. The Star of Unity was complete, its light blazing brighter than ever. With the Frozen Nebula restored and the final piece in place, the Starlight Sleigh's magic was nearly ready to shine again, its journey to save the cosmos entering its final chapter.

Chapter 4: The Starlight Sleigh Reborn

The Star of Unity shimmered in the heart of the Starlight Sleigh, its radiance filling the cosmos with a brilliance that had been absent for decades. Max and Clara gazed at it in awe, their faces bathed in its warm, golden light. The fragments they had retrieved had fused into a single, pulsing gem, glowing with the collective essence of giving, gratitude, love, and belief. For the first time since the sleigh's magic had faltered, Santa looked as though the weight of countless Christmases had lifted from his shoulders.

"We've done it," Santa said softly, his voice carrying both relief and pride. "The Star of Unity has been restored. The Starlight Sleigh can once again spread hope across the universe. But the final leg of the journey will not be easy."

As if to confirm his words, the sleigh shuddered violently, its glow dimming for an instant. Outside, the cosmos seemed to writhe and churn. Dark tendrils of energy twisted through the void, their movements chaotic and menacing. Santa's expression grew grave.

"That," he said, gesturing to the swirling maelstrom ahead, "is the Graviton Storm. It feeds on despair, doubt, and fear. For decades, the sleigh's absence allowed these emotions to fester, and now they've taken form, threatening to consume everything in their path. To return to Earth, we must navigate through it. But the sleigh's magic, while restored, is still fragile. It will take all of our combined strength to make it through."

Max swallowed hard, his earlier excitement tempered by the enormity of the task ahead. Clara, though equally nervous, placed a hand on his shoulder. "We've come this far," she said firmly. "We're not giving up now."

Santa nodded, his eyes filled with resolve. "Hold on tight. This will test us like nothing before."

The sleigh surged forward, its runners blazing with light as it entered the storm. Immediately, the temperature dropped, and the light of the Star of Unity seemed to flicker under the oppressive weight of the storm's despair. The dark tendrils lashed out, wrapping around the sleigh and pulling it off course.

Inside, the air grew heavy with an unshakable sense of hopelessness. Max felt it first—a voice in his mind whispering that he wasn't good enough, that his inventions were nothing more than childish dreams. Clara felt it too, a gnawing doubt that she wasn't strong or important enough to make a difference. Even Santa's usual steadiness seemed to waver, his shoulders slumping as the storm's oppressive energy took hold.

The sleigh groaned, its movements sluggish as the storm tightened its grip. The light of the Star of Unity dimmed further, its glow now barely visible. Clara clenched her fists, fighting the despair that clawed at her heart. "We can't let it win," she said, her voice trembling but defiant.

Max looked at her, the fire in her eyes sparking something deep within him. "She's right," he said, his voice rising above the storm's whispers. "This isn't who we are. We've faced challenges before, and we've come through them together. We can do this!"

Santa straightened, his determination reignited by their words. "The Star of Unity shines brightest when we believe in its light," he said. "Focus on hope, on the love and joy we've seen on this journey. The storm cannot overpower us if we stand united."

Max and Clara closed their eyes, drawing on the memories of their journey. They thought of Aurelia's test in the Realm of Giving, where they had learned the power of selfless generosity. They remembered the lessons of gratitude from Solara's maze and the warmth of love in Lumis's verdant realm. They called on the strength of belief they had found in Astra's trials and the courage they had shown in thawing the Ice Warden's heart.

The light of the Star of Unity began to brighten, its glow pushing back against the storm's darkness. The sleigh responded, its movements growing surer and faster. But the storm fought back, its tendrils lashing out with renewed fury, each strike a manifestation of the universe's lingering despair.

"We need more!" Clara shouted, her voice barely audible over the storm's howling.

Max's eyes lit up as an idea struck him. "The Star of Unity draws on belief, right?" he said, looking at Santa. "What if we amplify it? If we can channel our belief through the sleigh, maybe we can strengthen the Star's light enough to break through the storm!"

Santa nodded, his face lighting up with hope. "It's a risk, but it just might work. Max, use your ingenuity to guide the sleigh's magic. Clara, focus your heart on the light. Together, we can make this happen."

Max scrambled to the sleigh's control panel, his hands moving swiftly as he adjusted the crystalline levers and dials. Sparks of light danced across the sleigh's surface, responding to his touch. Clara closed her eyes, her hands gripping the edges of the sleigh as she poured every ounce of belief and hope she could muster into the Star.

The storm seemed to sense their growing strength and redoubled its efforts, its tendrils striking with greater force. The sleigh shook violently, and for a moment, it seemed as though the storm might win. But then, the Star of Unity blazed with a brilliance that rivaled the sun, its light cutting through the darkness like a beacon.

The tendrils dissolved, their despair unable to withstand the Star's radiance. The storm began to recede, its howls fading into silence as the sleigh surged forward, propelled by the combined strength of Max, Clara, and Santa.

As they emerged from the storm, the cosmos stretched before them, vast and glittering. The path to Earth was clear, and the sleigh's light shone brighter than ever. Santa turned to Max and Clara, his eyes shimmering with gratitude.

"You've done it," he said, his voice thick with emotion. "The Starlight Sleigh is reborn, not just because of the Star of Unity, but because of the hope and belief you've brought to it. The universe owes you a great debt."

Max and Clara exchanged a smile, their bond stronger than ever. They had faced the darkness and emerged victorious, proving that even in the darkest of times, hope could shine like a star.

As the sleigh descended toward Earth, its light bathed the planet in warmth and joy, rekindling the spirit of Christmas across the world. The legend of the Starlight Sleigh had been restored, and with it, the promise that no matter how dark the night, the light of hope would always find a way to shine.

Chapter 5: A Holiday Miracle Across the Stars

As the Starlight Sleigh descended toward Earth, its radiance lit up the night sky like a second sunrise. The Star of Unity, restored to its full brilliance, pulsed with an energy that seemed to resonate with every soul below. Across the cosmos, the journey of the sleigh brought more than just light; it carried a renewed sense of hope, joy, and connection that rippled through the hearts of all who gazed up in wonder.

Max and Clara sat side by side, the hum of the sleigh's magic beneath them like a soothing heartbeat. They were exhausted but exhilarated, their journey having tested every ounce of courage and belief they possessed. Santa, his crimson coat aglow with the light of the Star, turned to them with a look of deep pride and gratitude.

"You've done more than restore the Starlight Sleigh," he said, his voice carrying the warmth of countless Christmases. "You've reignited the true spirit of Christmas—unity, love, and hope—not just on Earth, but across the entire universe. This is a miracle that will be remembered for generations."

As the sleigh touched down in Evergreen Hollow, the small town was transformed. Snowflakes, infused with the magic of the Star of Unity, sparkled like tiny diamonds as they fell, blanketing the streets and rooftops in a shimmering frost. The townspeople, who had been preparing for the Christmas festival, paused to gaze in awe as the sleigh glided to a stop in the town square.

Children and adults alike gathered, their faces illuminated by the sleigh's ethereal glow. Whispers of disbelief spread through the crowd, turning to cheers of joy as Santa stepped down, his presence unmistakable. Behind him, Max and Clara followed, their hearts swelling with a mix of pride and humility.

"It's Santa!" a child exclaimed, their voice breaking the spell of silence.

"And Max and Clara!" another voice shouted.

The crowd surged forward, surrounding the trio with a mix of laughter, tears, and applause. Santa raised a hand, and the crowd quieted, hanging on his every word.

"Tonight marks the beginning of a new chapter in the story of Christmas," Santa began. "The Starlight Sleigh, once lost, has been restored, thanks to the bravery, ingenuity, and unwavering belief of two remarkable young heroes. Max and Clara didn't just save the sleigh—they reminded us all of the power of hope and the strength we find in one another."

The crowd erupted into cheers once more, and Clara found herself swept into a tight hug from Mrs. Whitmore, the town's baker, while Max was clapped on the back by Mr. Higgins, who rarely left his workshop but had come out to witness the miracle.

As the celebration unfolded, the sleigh began to hum softly, the Star of Unity sending pulses of light into the night sky. From Earth, the sleigh's magic spread outward, its energy traversing the cosmos. Across distant planets and star realms, beings paused in their tracks, looking up to see the light of the Star shining once more.

In the Realm of Giving, Aurelia smiled as the villagers they had helped saw their crops thrive under the glow of the restored sleigh. In the Realm of Gratitude, Solara watched the auroras dance brighter than ever, their golden hues reflected in the hearts of those who had found new purpose. Lumis in the Realm of Love felt the warmth of renewed connection spreading like sunlight, while Astra in the Realm of Belief observed the spark of faith returning to places long thought lost. Even the Ice Warden, now a radiant being of starlight, gazed upward from their transformed nebula with a sense of peace.

Back in Evergreen Hollow, the celebration reached its peak as Santa made an announcement that would change Max and Clara's lives forever. "Tonight, I appoint Max and Clara as honorary Guardians of the

Sleigh," he declared. "Their story will be told across the stars, inspiring future generations to believe in the magic of Christmas and the boundless power of hope."

Santa extended a hand, and a soft light enveloped Max and Clara, leaving them momentarily breathless. When the glow faded, each of them wore a small, star-shaped pin on their coats—a symbol of their new role. The crowd erupted into cheers, and the siblings exchanged a look of wonder and pride.

The night stretched into the early hours of Christmas morning, with songs, laughter, and shared stories filling the air. Max found himself answering endless questions about their journey, while Clara helped Mrs. Whitmore hand out freshly baked cookies infused with a touch of the sleigh's magic.

As dawn approached, Santa prepared to leave, the Starlight Sleigh now fully charged and ready to continue its mission of spreading joy across the universe. Max and Clara stood beside him, their hearts heavy with the bittersweet knowledge that their extraordinary journey was coming to an end.

"Will we ever see you again?" Clara asked, her voice tinged with emotion.

Santa smiled, his eyes twinkling like the Star itself. "Christmas is in your hearts now," he said. "And as Guardians of the Sleigh, you'll always be part of its story. This isn't an ending—it's just the beginning."

With that, he climbed into the sleigh, and with a final wave to the gathered crowd, it rose into the sky, leaving a trail of stardust in its wake. Max and Clara watched until it disappeared, the light of the Star of Unity a faint, glowing dot on the horizon.

As they returned home, the siblings couldn't help but marvel at how much had changed in just a few days. The once-forgotten barn now stood as a beacon of magic, its doors gleaming with the remnants of starlight. The town, too, seemed brighter, its spirit renewed by the miracle they had witnessed.

That Christmas morning, as the first rays of sunlight touched the snow-covered town, Max and Clara sat by their small fireplace, sipping cocoa and reflecting on the journey that had transformed their lives. They knew their story would be told and retold, not just in Evergreen Hollow but across the stars. And they knew, too, that the magic of the Starlight Sleigh would endure, shining as a beacon of hope in the darkest nights.

Christmas had been saved, but more importantly, its true meaning had been restored—not just for Earth, but for the entire universe. Max and Clara, the newest Guardians of the Sleigh, would carry that legacy forward, ensuring that the miracle of hope would never be forgotten.

Appendix A: The Realms of the Star of Unity

The journey of the Starlight Sleigh to restore the Star of Unity led Max, Clara, and Santa through four magical star realms, each embodying a vital aspect of the Christmas spirit. These realms are not just places but living embodiments of the energies that sustain the Star. Each realm provided unique challenges and invaluable lessons, shaping the heroes and deepening their understanding of the universe's interconnected magic. Below is a comprehensive exploration of these realms, their defining characteristics, and the profound truths they revealed.

1. The Realm of Giving

The first destination was the **Realm of Giving**, a vibrant nebula of golden and crimson hues that pulsed like a living heartbeat. The air in this realm hummed with an energy of generosity, and every star within its expanse glowed faintly, representing acts of kindness across the cosmos.

Upon arrival, Max and Clara found themselves in a crystalline village bathed in perpetual starlight. The villagers, though appearing to be ordinary beings, represented different facets of need—hunger, hardship, and longing for connection. The Keeper of Giving, **Aurelia**, a radiant figure cloaked in shifting robes that mirrored the dreams of others, tasked them with understanding true generosity.

The lesson of this realm was clear: giving is not about abundance but about providing what is truly needed. Through their thoughtful acts, Max and Clara restored the fragment of the Star, learning that the power of giving is measured by its impact on the receiver, not the size of the gift.

2. The Realm of Gratitude

The second realm was the **Realm of Gratitude**, an endless expanse of golden sands beneath an ever-shifting aurora of brilliant colors. The auroras reflected the gratitude of countless beings, their intensity growing or fading based on the strength of appreciation in the hearts of those they touched.

Here, the Keeper of Gratitude, **Solara**, presented Max and Clara with a maze of mirrors. Each mirror reflected their doubts, fears, and insecurities, challenging them to navigate its shifting corridors. The maze was both literal and metaphorical, designed to teach them the importance of acknowledging and appreciating their strengths, even in the face of their flaws.

The fragment of the Star hidden here represented the enduring power of gratitude to transform even the bleakest situations. By expressing genuine appreciation for their own resilience and each other's support, Max and Clara uncovered the fragment, learning that gratitude is the foundation of inner strength and connection.

3. The Realm of Love

A stark contrast to the icy isolation of the Frozen Nebula, the **Realm of Love** was a verdant paradise, alive with warmth and connection. Towering trees with leaves that shimmered like diamonds stretched toward a sky of soft pink and gold, while gentle creatures roamed freely, their presence exuding comfort and acceptance.

The Keeper of Love, **Lumis**, a serene figure wrapped in glowing vines, guided the siblings through this realm. Here, the challenge was deeply personal: to confront their insecurities and learn to love themselves as they were. Max grappled with his fear of failure, while Clara faced her lingering doubts about her importance.

In embracing their imperfections and finding strength in their bond, Max and Clara unlocked the fragment hidden in the heart of the realm.

They learned that love begins within and radiates outward, creating unbreakable connections that transcend distance and time.

4. The Realm of Belief

The final realm was the most challenging: the **Realm of Belief**, a stark, otherworldly landscape where shifting shadows and piercing light clashed in a chaotic dance. This realm existed at the intersection of doubt and faith, embodying the constant struggle between fear and trust.

The Keeper of Belief, **Astra**, a luminous figure with an ever-changing form, challenged the trio to hold fast to hope even as illusions sought to shatter their resolve. They faced visions of failure, darkness, and despair, each designed to erode their belief in themselves and their mission.

Through sheer determination and the strength of their bond, Max and Clara found the fragment, learning that belief is the foundation of all magic. Without it, the light of the Star of Unity could never shine, and the magic of Christmas would falter.

Cosmic Map of the Realms

(Visuals can be imagined or illustrated.)

In the cosmos, the realms form a symbolic constellation surrounding the Frozen Nebula, where the Star of Unity was originally forged. Each realm aligns with a cardinal direction:

- **North**: The Realm of Gratitude, glowing golden like a celestial compass.
- **South**: The Realm of Love, radiating warmth and vibrant color.
- **East**: The Realm of Belief, its shifting lights and shadows visible from afar.
- **West**: The Realm of Giving, pulsing like the heart of the cosmos.

At the center lies the **Frozen Nebula**, a once-dormant expanse transformed by the heroes' journey. This alignment reflects the balance of the Christmas spirit, with the Star of Unity at its heart.

The Realms of the Star of Unity serve as a reminder that the true magic of Christmas lies in the strength of the human (and cosmic) spirit. Each represents an essential facet of a universe in harmony, and their restoration ensures that the light of hope, joy, and unity will shine brightly for all eternity.

Appendix B: The Mechanics of the Starlight Sleigh

The **Starlight Sleigh** is not merely a vehicle—it is a marvel of celestial engineering, combining ancient magic and advanced cosmic technology. Forged from the remnants of a dying star, it embodies the spirit of unity, designed to traverse the infinite expanse of the universe while spreading joy and hope. Below is an in-depth exploration of the sleigh's magical workings, its systems, and the unique features that make it the most powerful and extraordinary mode of transportation in existence.

1. The Star of Unity: The Heart of the Sleigh

At the core of the Starlight Sleigh lies the **Star of Unity**, a celestial gem that acts as both its power source and guiding light. The Star draws its energy from the collective belief, love, and hope of all beings in the universe. This makes the sleigh's power intrinsically tied to the spirit of Christmas—when joy and unity flourish, the Star shines brightest.

The Star's functions include:

- **Energy Generation**: It powers the sleigh's propulsion system, enabling it to transcend space and time.
- **Emotional Resonance**: The Star emits pulses of magic that amplify hope and joy wherever the sleigh travels.
- **Barrier Protection**: Its energy creates a protective shield around the sleigh, allowing it to withstand cosmic phenomena such as black holes, solar flares, and interstellar storms.
- **Healing Aura**: The Star's magic can restore balance and harmony to realms affected by despair or darkness, as seen during the restoration of the Frozen Nebula.

2. Cosmic Navigation System

The Starlight Sleigh's navigation system is a blend of advanced starmaps and intuitive magical guidance, ensuring precise travel across the vast and unpredictable cosmos.

- **The Celestial Compass**: A glowing orb embedded in the sleigh's dashboard, the compass projects a holographic map of the universe. It syncs with the Star of Unity to highlight the sleigh's destination, adjusting for cosmic shifts in real-time.
- **The Constellation Pathway**: The sleigh generates trails of stardust that form constellations visible only to the sleigh's pilot, marking the safest and most direct routes through space.
- **Instinctive Guidance**: The Star of Unity enhances the intuition of the pilot, helping Santa navigate through unpredictable anomalies such as the Graviton Storm.

3. Propulsion and Flight Mechanics

The sleigh's propulsion system combines the raw energy of the Star of Unity with intricate rune-forged mechanisms.

- **Stellar Runners**: The sleigh's runners are not ordinary metal but a cosmic alloy etched with ancient runes that glow when activated. These runners glide seamlessly through snow, air, and even the vacuum of space, adapting to the terrain.
- **Stardust Drives**: Located beneath the sleigh, these drives convert the Star's energy into thrust, allowing the sleigh to accelerate to light speeds and beyond.
- **Time-Warp Thrusters**: Special boosters at the rear of the sleigh enable short bursts of time dilation, allowing Santa to deliver gifts across the universe in a single night.

4. Unique Features

The Starlight Sleigh is equipped with a variety of magical and practical features, making it unparalleled in versatility and capability.

- **Gift Chambers**: Hidden compartments beneath the sleigh's seating store an infinite array of gifts, organized through a magical inventory system that ensures the right gift reaches the right recipient.
- **Aurora Cloak**: A shimmering shield that envelopes the sleigh in a veil of auroras, rendering it invisible to the naked eye and protecting it from hostile entities.
- **Emotion Amplifier**: The sleigh's presence heightens the feelings of joy and wonder in those who see it, spreading the magic of Christmas wherever it travels.
- **Memory Keeper**: A device embedded in the sleigh's framework that records the stories and lessons of its journeys, ensuring they are preserved for future generations.

5. Glossary of Terms and Tools

- **Star of Unity**: The magical gem that powers the sleigh, embodying the core values of Christmas—giving, gratitude, love, and belief.
- **Celestial Compass**: A magical navigation tool projecting starmaps and guiding the sleigh through the cosmos.
- **Stellar Runners**: Sleigh components made from cosmic alloys that enable seamless travel across any terrain.
- **Stardust Drives**: Energy converters that transform the Star's magic into propulsion.
- **Time-Warp Thrusters**: Mechanisms allowing the sleigh to bend time for faster delivery.
- **Aurora Cloak**: A protective and concealing shield of auroras.

- **Emotion Amplifier**: A feature that spreads joy and wonder, enhancing the holiday spirit.
- **Memory Keeper**: A recording device that chronicles the sleigh's journeys for posterity.
- **Graviton Storm**: A cosmic phenomenon fueled by despair and doubt, posing significant danger to the sleigh.

The **Starlight Sleigh** is not just a machine; it is a symbol of unity and hope, intricately designed to bridge the gap between realms and hearts. Its restoration marks the rekindling of the Christmas spirit, proving that no matter how dark the universe may seem, light and magic can always find a way to shine.

<u>Message from the Author:</u>

I hope you enjoyed this book, I love astrology and knew there was not a book such as this out on the shelf. I love metaphysical items as well. Please check out my other books:

-Life of Government Benefits

-My life of Hell

-My life with Hydrocephalus

-Red Sky

-World Domination:Woman's rule

-World Domination:Woman's Rule 2: The War

-Life and Banishment of Apophis: book 1

-The Kidney Friendly Diet

-The Ultimate Hemp Cookbook

-Creating a Dispensary(legally)

-Cleanliness throughout life: the importance of showering from childhood to adulthood.

-Strong Roots: The Risks of Overcoddling children

-Hemp Horoscopes: Cosmic Insights and Earthly Healing

- Celestial Hemp Navigating the Zodiac: Through the Green Cosmos

-Astrological Hemp: Aligning The Stars with Earth's Ancient Herb

-The Astrological Guide to Hemp: Stars, Signs, and Sacred Leaves

-Green Growth: Innovative Marketing Strategies for your Hemp Products and Dispensary

-Cosmic Cannabis

-Astrological Munchies

-Henry The Hemp

-Zodiacal Roots: The Astrological Soul Of Hemp

- **Green Constellations: Intersection of Hemp and Zodiac**

-Hemp in The Houses: An astrological Adventure Through The Cannabis Galaxy

-Galactic Ganja Guide

Heavenly Hemp

Zodiac Leaves

Doctor Who Astrology

Cannastrology

Stellar Satvias and Cosmic Indicas

Celestial Cannabis: A Zodiac Journey

AstroHerbology: The Sky and The Soil: Volume 1

AstroHerbology:Celestial Cannabis:Volume 2

Cosmic Cannabis Cultivation

The Starry Guide to Herbal Harmony: Volume 1

The Starry Guide to Herbal Harmony: Cannabis Universe: Volume 2

Yugioh Astrology: Astrological Guide to Deck, Duels and more

Nightmare Mansion: Echoes of The Abyss

Nightmare Mansion 2: Legacy of Shadows

Nightmare Mansion 3: Shadows of the Forgotten

Nightmare Mansion 4: Echoes of the Damned

The Life and Banishment of Apophis: Book 2

Nightmare Mansion: Halls of Despair

Healing with Herb: Cannabis and Hydrocephalus

Planetary Pot: Aligning with Astrological Herbs: Volume 1

Fast Track to Freedom: 30 Days to Financial Independence Using AI, Assets, and Agile Hustles

Cosmic Hemp Pathways

How to Become Financially Free in 30 Days: 10,000 Paths to Prosperity

Zodiacal Herbage: Astrological Insights: Volume 1

Nightmare Mansion: Whispers in the Walls

The Daleks Invade Atlantis

Henry the hemp and Hydrocephalus

10X The Kidney Friendly Diet

Cannabis Universe: Adult coloring book

Hemp Astrology: The Healing Power of the Stars

Zodiacal Herbage: Astrological Insights: Cannabis Universe: Volume 2

<u>**Planetary Pot: Aligning with Astrological Herbs: Cannabis Universes: Volume 2**</u>

Doctor Who Meets the Replicators and SG-1: The Ultimate Battle for Survival

Nightmare Mansion: Curse of the Blood Moon

<u>**The Celestial Stoner: A Guide to the Zodiac**</u>

Cosmic Pleasures: Sex Toy Astrology for Every Sign

Hydrocephalus Astrology: Navigating the Stars and Healing Waters

Lapis and the Mischievous Chocolate Bar

Celestial Positions: Sexual Astrology for Every Sign

Apophis's Shadow Work Journal: : A Journey of Self-Discovery and Healing

Kinky Cosmos: Sexual Kink Astrology for Every Sign

Digital Cosmos: The Astrological Digimon Compendium

Stellar Seeds: The Cosmic Guide to Growing with Astrology

Apophis's Daily Gratitude Journal

Cat Astrology: Feline Mysteries of the Cosmos

The Cosmic Kama Sutra: An Astrological Guide to Sexual Positions

Unleash Your Potential: A Guided Journal Powered by AI Insights

Whispers of the Enchanted Grove

Cosmic Pleasures: An Astrological Guide to Sexual Kinks

369, 12 Manifestation Journal

Whisper of the nocturne journal(blank journal for writing or drawing)

The Boogey Book

Locked In Reflection: A Chastity Journey Through Locktober

Generating Wealth Quickly:

How to Generate $100,000 in 24 Hours

Star Magic: Harness the Power of the Universe

The Flatulence Chronicles: A Fart Journal for Self-Discovery

The Doctor and The Death Moth

Seize the Day: A Personal Seizure Tracking Journal

The Ultimate Boogeyman Safari: A Journey into the Boogie World and Beyond

Whispers of Samhain: 1,000 Spells of Love, Luck, and Lunar Magic: Samhain Spell Book

Apophis's guides:

Witch's Spellbook Crafting Guide for Halloween

<u>Frost & Flame: The Enchanted Yule Grimoire of 1000 Winter Spells</u>

<u>The Ultimate Boogey Goo Guide & Spooky Activities for Halloween Fun</u>

Harmony of the Scales: A Libra's Spellcraft for Balance and Beauty

The Enchanted Advent: 36 Days of Christmas Wonders

Nightmare Mansion: The Labyrinth of Screams

Harvest of Enchantment: 1,000 Spells of Gratitude, Love, and Fortune for Thanksgiving

The Boogey Chronicles: A Journal of Nightly Encounters and Shadowy Secrets

The 12 Days of Financial Freedom: A Step-by-Step Christmas Countdown to Transform Your Finances

Sigil of the Eternal Spiral Blank Journal

A Christmas Feast: Timeless Recipes for Every Meal

Holiday Stress-Free Solutions: A Survival Guide to Thriving During the Festive Season

Yu-Gi-Oh! Holiday Gifting Mastery: The Ultimate Guide for Fans and Newcomers Alike

Holiday Harmony: A Hydrocephalus Survival Guide for the Festive Season

Celestial Craft: The Witch's Almanac for 2025 – A Cosmic Guide to Manifestations, Moons, and Mystical Events

Doctor Who: The Toymaker's Winter Wonderland

Tulsa King Unveiled: A Thrilling Guide to Stallone's Mafia Masterpiece

Pendulum Craft: A Complete Guide to Crafting and Using Personalized Divination Tools

Nightmare Mansion: Santa's Eternal Eve

Starlight Noel: A Cosmic Journey through Christmas Mysteries

The Dark Architect: Unlocking the Blueprint of Existence

Surviving the Embrace: The Ultimate Guide to Encounters with The Hugging Molly

The Enchanted Codex: Secrets of the Craft for Witches, Wiccans, and Pagans

Harvest of Gratitude: A Complete Thanksgiving Guide

Yuletide Essentials: A Complete Guide to an Authentic and Magical Christmas

Celestial Smokes: A Cosmic Guide to Cigars and Astrology

Living in Balance: A Comprehensive Survival Guide to Thriving with Diabetes Insipidus

Cosmic Symbiosis: The Venom Zodiac Chronicles

The Cursed Paw of Ambition

Cosmic Symbiosis: The Astrological Venom Journal

Celestial Wonders Unfold: A Stargazer's Guide to the Cosmos (2024-2029)

The Ultimate Black Friday Prepper's Guide: Mastering Shopping Strategies and Savings

Cosmic Sales: The Astrological Guide to Black Friday Shopping

Legends of the Corn Mother and Other Harvest Myths

Whispers of the Harvest: The Corn Mother's Journal

The Evergreen Spellbook

The Doctor Meets the Boogeyman

The White Witch of Rose Hall's SpellBook

The Gingerbread Golem's Shadow: A Study in Sweet Darkness

The Gingerbread Golem Codex: An Academic Exploration of Sweet Myths

The Gingerbread Golem Grimoire: Sweet Magicks and Spells for the Festive Witch

The Curse of the Gingerbread Golem

10-minute Christmas Crafts for kids

<u>Christmas Crisis Solutions: The Ultimate Last-Minute Survival Guide</u>

Gingerbread Golem Recipes: Holiday Treats with a Magical Twist

The Infinite Key: Unlocking Mystical Secrets of the Ages

Enchanted Yule: A Wiccan and Pagan Guide to a Magical and Memorable Season

Dinosaurs of Power: Unlocking Ancient Magick

Astro-Dinos: The Cosmic Guide to Prehistoric Wisdom

Gallifrey's Yule Logs: A Festive Doctor Who Cookbook

The Dino Grimoire: Secrets of Prehistoric Magick

The Gift They Never Knew They Needed

The Gingerbread Golem's Culinary Alchemy: Enchanting Recipes for a Sweetly Dark Feast

A Time Lord Christmas: Holiday Adventures with the Doctor

Krampusproofing Your Home: Defensive Strategies for Yule

Silent Frights: A Collection of Christmas Creepypastas to Chill Your Bones

Santa Raptor's Jolly Carnage: A Dino-Claus Christmas Tale

Prehistoric Palettes: A Dino Wicca Coloring Journey

The Christmas Wishkeeper Chronicles

If you want solar for your home go here: https://www.harborso-lar.live/apophisenterprises/

Get Some Tarot cards: https://www.makeplayingcards.com/sell/
apophis-occult-shop

Get   some   shirts: https://www.bonfire.com/store/apophis-shirt-emporium/

<u>Instagrams:</u>
@apophis_enterprises,
@apophisbookemporium,
@apophisscardshop
Twitter: @apophisenterpr1
Tiktok:@apophisenterprise
Youtube: @sg1fan23477, @FiresideRetreatKingdom
Hive: @sg1fan23477
CheeLee: @SG1fan23477

Podcast: Apophis Chat Zone: https://open.spotify.com/show/5zXbrCLEV2xzCp8ybrfHsk?si=fb4d4fdbdce44dec

Newsletter: https://apophiss-newsletter-27c897.beehiiv.com/

If you want to support me or see posts of other projects that I have come over to: **buymeacoffee.com/mpetchinskg**
I post there daily several times a day

Get your Dinowicca or Christmas themed digital products, especially Santa Raptor songs and other musics. Here: **https://sg1fan23477.gumroad.com**

Apophis Yuletide Digital has not only digital Christmas items, but it will have all things with Dinowicca as well as other Digital products.

www.ingramcontent.com/pod-product-compliance
Lightning Source LLC
Chambersburg PA
CBHW061728130726
47996CB00006B/2547